FEAST

TANZANIA GLOVER

I

Cover Art by Scheba Derogene

TANZANIA GLOVER

www.tanzaniaglover.com

Booking With Love
332 S Michigan Ave
Suite #121- 2217
Chicago, IL 60604
www.bookingwithlove.com

To all the girls whose bodies developed faster than their minds could. Put the burdens below and behind you because they were never yours to carry. It wasn't your fault.

TANZANIA GLOVER

THE APPETIZER

Before thirteen I was too young to know that some compliments came with ulterior motives so of course it used to flatter me when I was called mature for my age. After thirteen though, I was finally mature enough to understand that "mature" was just code for *ready to babysit* from women and *ready to fuck* from men.

Moe had just been three years older than me then though so I knew she really meant it when she said I looked and seemed the same age as her. Going in I'd been a complete skeptic because I definitely didn't need another "Big Sis" or mentor so soon, but my foster mother at the time insisted I at least give it a try since she worked for the Chicago branch of the organization.

She praised their ability to match Littles and Bigs based on shared interests, but even back then I could tell the only criteria used to put Little Lee Williams and Big Monica McGhee together was that we were the only two black faces in a sea of white, beige and brown. Ultimately they weren't wrong though because we did hit it off right away.

For one she loved Bros4Lyfe and Orrin Greenwood just as much if not more than I did. Eventually her bedroom became my favorite place in the world because the walls were covered in posters and she had all their CDs. She was even the one to take me to my first concert for my fourteenth birthday where I screamed so much I couldn't speak for days.

I knew that she'd only signed up to be a Big for her college applications, but by the time I started high school with her at Kenwood we were so close that she would lie and tell people that I was her adopted little sister. A part of me loved it because Moe would've been the best sister a girl could ask for.

Plus after being in the system for a while by then I'd accepted that I would probably never know what it was like to actually be adopted. But a bigger part of me hated it because as much as I would've loved to be a part of the beautiful McGhee clan of Hyde Park, back then I'd have preferred to become one a different way.

When Moe first mentioned having a twin I'd imagined a Tia and Tamera type of bond complete with funny stories about trading places, but she just laughed at my assumption before telling me that her twin was a boy.

The first time I saw Monte I knew he would be my first. Up until that point I had been decidedly wary of all members of the opposite sex, but there was just something about him that disarmed and undermined my typical state of avoidance.

As expected he was just as pretty as Moe was, but his tall athletic build, the hint of a mustache above his naturally curled lips, and of course the fact that he had a penis made me appreciate their shared beauty even more on him.

It seemed like his mind wasn't too far behind mine after being introduced because the second he thought I was out of earshot he was giving Moe the third degree about me.

"She got a boyfriend?"

"You'll be in handcuffs before you can even get your pants down. That's my Little and she just turned thirteen."

"Quit playing. Ain't nothing little or thirteen about that girl," he said in disbelief before making a lewd remark about the size of my breasts and behind.

Their exchange naturally stayed with me for years because

it had sparked the beginning of Moe putting me up on game about boys. She must've seen the twinkle in my eye when I looked at him because when he left she very bluntly told me to stay away from niggas like him.

"They're never on shit and they think running through girls is cute," she'd warned, but it fell on deaf ears for a while.

Still more naïve than I knew then, I figured Moe badmouthing her brother was probably some type of sibling rivalry until I personally got to witness him being a hoe during my first but his final year of high school.

Every single one of his

conquests, even friends of ours that Moe had also warned, thought that they would be the one to change him, but the second he got what he wanted he would be gone with the wind like Clark Gable.

When I was still in my delusional, crushing hard phase I was flat out jealous of the crumbs of attention that he fed to other girls, but after a while I just laughed at them right along with Moe. Sure I was no better because I still secretly lusted after his fine ass too, but the difference was that by the time I made it to their age I had enough sense to know he would never change.

And it didn't bother me any by then because changing him wasn't what I wanted anymore. What I wanted was just to finally get my turn.

And I was sure I would've eventually gotten it too if it wasn't for Moe's meddling ass finally putting her foot down about him going after her friends. But I suppose that it was a necessary boundary after he caused an all-out brawl and uncomfortable living situation from bouncing back and forth between her roommates.

Meanwhile I was still being bounced from home to home, never really staying anywhere longer than six months for one reason or another. We didn't let the circumstances come between us though. Dawson University was only a forty minute train ride away from the city so I visited her on campus as often as I could.

The lady I stayed with for my last year of high school cared more about the checks from the state than my curfew so she never even bothered to ask where I slept when I wasn't there some weekends. But the swinging door of bad foster parents was just about in my rearview by that point so I continued to keep my head in the books and didn't let anything distract me from becoming a Dawson Demon right along with Moe.

I missed valedictorian by a nose, but the important thing was that I'd managed to get a diploma at all since the odds stacked against me had been just as tough as they were tall. As my salutatorian speech came to a close and I said farewell to the class of 2009, I saw one familiar but unexpected face in the back of the crowd cheering for me harder than anybody.

Back when Moe had asked for two graduation tickets I'd assumed it would be her mama tagging along since she'd always been so nice and welcoming to my Orphan Annie ass, but instead there was a different McGhee proudly sitting beside her.

And since I'd never had a reason to hug him before there was nothing to compare it to, but still the way Monte held on to my newly emancipated and eighteen year old body told me that his ability to keep his promise to Moe was about to get tested like never before.

Or so I'd thought.

I couldn't remember what exactly had convinced me that he would begin to see me in a whole new light once I started at Dawson, but he continued paying me the same amount of attention as when I was thirteen and he first realized that he couldn't have me. There was one new layer to our relationship though and it kept me up some nights wondering about what it really meant.

Because of the obvious mutual attraction we'd never bothered pretending to treat each other like siblings the way Moe and I did, but literally the second I stepped foot on campus he suddenly started hovering and treating me like I was a little kid. Not letting me have more than a drink or two at parties, insisting that I call him or Moe for a ride if I was out alone after dark, and of course scaring potentials off.

But then again he had been running romantic interference even back when I was still just visiting. Like one time when one of his fine frat brothers was a little too geeked to be in my face only I didn't mind at all since he was cute enough to make me forget Monte was even in the function.

His name was Byron, but I was right in the middle of finding out why people were calling him Biggs when Monte swooped in to break it all up.

"Ayo move around, B. She still got milk on her tongue."

"Shit, I'm tryna be some milk

then."

And even with how embarrassed I'd been then, I would have killed for it to happen again since I barely got any action to be interrupted these days. It was so weird. Back when I was visiting, I couldn't pry them off my bra strap, but now every cutie I came across seemed to just look but keep their distance.

Even the couple that I had managed to sneak and talk to behind Monte's back barely wanted to speak when they saw me now and I couldn't figure out why because nothing about me had changed. In fact the more effort I seemed to put into my looks the less attention I got. And it wasn't like I had tied all my worth to how many boys wanted me, but still it felt like I was in *The Twilight Zone*.

Normally it would have been easy to forget about them and throw myself into school like I'd always done, but for the first time ever I had a class with Monte. He'd put off taking Psych 101 until he couldn't anymore so now he was sitting beside me every Monday, Wednesday and Friday. And because I'd just aced the AP exam of course I used the opportunity to get some alone time by becoming his tutor.

He was actually pretty smart

when he wanted to be, but I knew from Moe that he'd taken a recent messy situation between their parents pretty hard and he'd missed a full week of classes. Midterms were right around the corner though so I wasn't surprised when he enlisted my help to get him caught up and ready for the exam.

"C'mon, you know this. Maslow. Hierarchy of Needs," I said after trying to draw him back in since neither one of us had been able to concentrate much for the better part of an hour.

Him because his mind was elsewhere and me because we were alone in the off campus apartment that he shared with Moe and I couldn't help but wonder if he was wearing any boxers underneath his basketball shorts.

"Okay think about it like this. Sex is high on your priority list, right?" I asked attempting to both get his attention and to finally get him talking to me like an adult for once.

"Wait what?" he asked suddenly sitting up just like I knew he would.

"Just answer the question. It is, right?" He blankly nodded. "Right, but let's say you didn't have a place to live or food to eat. Where do you think you would rank it then?"

"Number one," he blurted out with zero hesitation.

"Even over food and shelter?"

"Yeah. When you got dick like mine, somebody is always trying to feed and fuck you so I'll be alright."

"Can you at least pretend to take this seriously?" I asked as he sighed then played in the overgrown hair on his face.

He'd been long overdue for a shapeup and a shave, but his genes were so blessed that even his hobo chic state couldn't detract from them.

"My fault. I'm not really feeling this right now so you can

go if you want or wait for Moe in her room."

"Well just kick me out then," I said pretending to be hurt. "And speaking of getting fed, I thought you were supposed to be buying me dinner for helping you study on a Friday night."

"Yeah but how much studying actually took place though?" he asked trying to weasel his way out of it before I threatened to take my notes right out the door with me.

I told him I was craving pizza so I assumed that we would hit up everybody's favorite spot right up the street until he suggested getting it delivered since he didn't feel like running into anybody. I already knew the reason but still found myself asking why his mood had suddenly been as dreary as the fall weather we'd been having.

"You don't have to front. I know Moe told you about what's going on at home," he said somberly before looking down at his interlocked fingers.

And he was right. Moe had told me all about how the stork would soon be adding a member to the Hyde Park Huxtables only the newest bundle of joy had nothing to do with their mama and everything to do with their daddy getting sloppy with his cheating. Moe was obviously upset at the whole situation too, but Monte seemed to be taking the betrayal more personally than even Mrs. McGhee was.

"Yeah I was sorry to hear about it, but at least they're gonna try to work through it, right?" I offered to sound hopeful, but it just made him roll his eyes.

"What's to work through? He let us all down, but my mama is too weak to even fake like she might leave," he said while shaking his head like he still couldn't believe what was happening.

Not knowing what else to say on the subject, I spread my arms for a hug, but he just smiled and insisted that it wasn't necessary.

"Monte, come here. I'm not just Moe's friend. I'm yours too and you look like you really need one."

I quickly jumped up to stand in front of him then bent to lift him off the couch since he was still acting like a grump.

"Alright. Alright," he relented after I grunted from struggling to get him up. When he was finally on his feet, I slid my arms under his which made him have to wrap me up in a bear hug.

"Ay I thought this was supposed to be my hug," he

playfully complained as he rested his chin on top of my head.

"It's both of ours," I assured him while shamelessly snuggling into his chest. He mostly smelled like laundry detergent and soap, but the pheromones from his skin were coming through pretty strong too.

"I've lowkey been wanting to do this again since my graduation anyway. I can't believe you've been keeping these good hugs all to yourself for years when I needed them. Stingy ass."

We shared a quick, innocent laugh, but I heard his begin to fade when I attempted to turn the embrace from friendly to *friendlier.* I'd given myself permission to slide my fingertips under his wifebeater to gently rub his lower back, but he quickly stopped me to pull back and peer down into my eyes. He studied them for a few, still seconds before the cutest smile crept up on his face.

"Ay stop playing with me, Lee. Moe put you up to this to test me, didn't she?" he asked as he looked around like there was a hidden camera somewhere.

"No. This test was all my idea," I swore as I stepped to him again and to really let him know how serious I was I let my hardening nipples press into him this time. "You know I've been waiting for you and I know you've been waiting for me too."

His eyebrow raising in consideration made me sure that my seduction attempt was going off without a hitch, but him suddenly grabbing me by the chin like I was a disobedient kid let me know I'd showed my hand too soon.

"Don't ever do no shit like that again. You're a little ass girl to me and you need to learn to stay in a child's place," he spat through gritted teeth even though I could feel his body tensing up with both anger and lust.

"A child's place?" I echoed in disbelief because he'd been staring holes into said child's backside for as long as I'd known him.

"Monte, you're barely old enough to drink and your mama still has your birth certificate so relax about three years, grandpa. Plus your parents have a way bigger age gap."

"Yeah and how's that working out for them right about now?" he retorted before finally separating our bodies with a small push to get me and my titties out of his space for good.

"Fuck you," I spat more out of humiliation than anything as I quickly grabbed my coat and bag then stomped over to the door.

"Maybe when you're a little older," he offered with a wink just to dig the knife in deeper before slapping my butt so hard I nearly jumped out of my skin.

I wanted nothing more than to turn around and return the favor to his face, but I was stunned to see Moe on the other side of the door I'd already opened. Thankfully her head had been down looking for her keys so she didn't catch us, but she was obviously confused at my presence even before me trying to rush out in a hurry.

"Was I supposed to be

meeting you here?" she asked with her brow arched in the same way her evil twin's just had.

"No. Monte just needed me to drop off my psych notes for the midterm," I said trying to sound as normal as possible, but I knew refusing to look back at him was making me look guilty so I finally turned then stepped aside to let her inside.

"I thought I told you to stop letting his dumb butt copy off you. He wants to miss class? Let him stay and be a super senior so I can get solo graduation gifts for once," she joked before sticking out her tongue as he flipped her the bird then went for his wallet.

I was almost out the door without Moe suspecting anything when Monte stopped me to slide some cash in my hand. Then it was my turn to be confused especially because he definitely held on longer than he needed to in order to further taunt me.

"What's this for?"

"For the pizza I owe you. And go straight home after you get it because it's getting dark," he said in an unusually teasing tone which I saw caught Moe's attention too.

I couldn't react the way I wanted to so I just thanked him before saying goodnight to them both then hightailing it out of there. I was so embarrassed and paranoid about the whole situation that I barely talked to Moe for the rest of the weekend.

I wasn't sure if or when Monte would rat me out for coming on to him so I debated whether I would just tell her myself to get ahead of him. I *was* sure that it wouldn't be a big deal to her because obviously it wasn't a secret that I used to have a crush on him back in the day, but I still didn't want to disappoint her by ultimately being just another stupid girl under Monte's spell.

Moe had never tried to control me and she treated me like an equal from day one, but she also loved that I wasn't thirsty or boy crazy like some girls my age and she encouraged me to abstain for as long as possible.

"Lee, most of these niggas don't even deserve to know what pussy smells like so keep waiting their asses out."

And that had pretty much been the plan until the opportunity to do the opposite finally presented itself. Looking back over everything though, it had actually been for the best that Monte rejected me since Moe unexpectedly coming home early would've definitely gotten us caught in the act.

The most bizarre part though was that come Monday morning in class it was like nothing had ever happened. He just thanked me for loaning him my notes then made small talk like usual until our professor walked in.

I'd been expecting a much more awkward first exchange, but following his lead and avoiding talking about it made things go smoothly from that point forward. In fact if it wasn't for how much I still cringed every time I replayed it, I would have questioned if I'd just imagined it all.

Because he still fixed my laptop every time it caught a

virus from stealing all the music Limewire had to offer. He still didn't care that I was always the one to mess up his Netflix DVD queue getting rom coms delivered. He even still let me borrow his car whenever Moe was busy or off campus seeing her boyfriend.

And since he was the last person on Earth still holding onto MySpace I took note that I hadn't yet lost my third place spot in his Top 8 behind rapper Wayne East and Moe respectively. Yeah he was still being regular ass Monte and doing everything I wanted him to do except for fucking me.

But I guess I was in good

company since it seemed like he hadn't been fucking anybody. I was more relieved than I realized when Moe joked that he must've finally caught something he couldn't get rid of since he hadn't brought anybody back to their place in weeks.

In a slightly suspicious tone she asked if I'd noticed anything different with him and after adding my own joke about Little Monte finally giving out from exhaustion, I reminded her that he was more than likely just really disappointed in their dad and realizing that sleeping around without a care in the world had consequences.

And thinking of it that way made me finally look at our situation from his point of view. While not acknowledging my colossal blunder had been an even bigger blow to my confidence than the initial rejection, ultimately I understood why he'd done it and I began to put the whole thing behind me.

It didn't stay there for too long though because unfortunately for Monte, Homecoming weekend at DU would bring more than alumni back to campus. He had been a shell of himself for weeks by then, but Moe figured he would at least snap out of it for his brothers in royal blue.

Dawson was far from an HBCU, but that didn't stop the Black alumni, especially Divine Nine members, from showing up and out every year. And I knew the Sigmas would be even more obnoxious than usual since Lil' Wayne had practically become an honorary member after shouting them out on a song with that one kid from Degrassi.

Still Monte decided to keep on wallowing in his worry and skip the big bash, but since I'd decided to get my mind off him once and for all I didn't pay it any mind. Tired of feeling ignored by everybody, I got Moe to help me find a head turning but not bank breaking dress to remind me who the hell I was. I still thought it was super ironic that she'd been the one to teach me how to shop on a budget when I didn't know how she'd managed to even learn since her family was paid and had the best of everything.

And even though the little black dress had been cheap, it made me look and feel like a million bucks so I knew I would finally be getting the attention that I so desperately craved. To add to the look I pressed my natural hair out then added barrel curls to the ends. I also traded in my Pastries for cute heels but made sure that my lip gloss was still popping. Nobody could tell me that I looked like anything less than a mature woman for the night.

Monte had left to work out before Moe and I finished getting ready at their apartment, but I'd told myself that I was no longer trying to literally or figuratively get a rise out of him so I didn't care if he'd seen my transformation or not. Besides I had a new, *bigger* target in mind again and I set my sights on him the second I stepped into the surprisingly lavish party.

I figured I'd gotten rejected once and lived to talk about it so I could definitely do it again especially since without Monte around to block this time Biggs and I could finally get back to what we'd started on my visit. I barely had to scan the crowd of well-dressed dancing bodies before immediately finding him standing by the refreshments.

Before walking over we did the mutual Black nod of acknowledgment that I'd quickly come to realize was a requirement at all PWIs. Always the life of the party, he asked if I wanted something to drink and I graciously accepted.

"You got any milk? Chocolate is my favorite," I said forwardly calling back to our last interaction then watched his cheeks swell into a smile, but it didn't lead to anything else after he discreetly handed me a glass of something clear from the open bar for those with wristbands.

After a while of standing there twiddling my thumbs and making small talk about the food and music, I asked him if he wanted to dance to get us moving and back to how we were before, but to my surprise he declined, claiming that he was tired and taking a break from strolling.

My face nearly cracked like a windshield before I decided to check my breath then come right out and ask him what was going on. I knew better than to make a man tell me twice that he didn't want me, but I refused to walk away without finally finding out why every male on this campus seemed to suddenly be immune to my charms.

He dramatically set his drink down before turning to me.

"Look I ain't like these other niggas in here. I don't share or fuck behind my brothers," he said with misplaced conviction after nodding over to a few of the dancing Black boys in blue.

"Oh...kay. But what does that have to do with me? I'm not with a Sigma," I said through an awkward laugh until he gave me a disbelieving look that I promptly returned.

"So you and P not fucking?" he asked looking square in my eyes like he was daring me to lie to him.

Obviously I wouldn't have been lying, but I couldn't even muster up a convincing expression because it took a minute to even realize who he'd meant. I didn't know any Sigmas whose name began with the letter P, but Monte's line name just so happened to be Python.

"Hell no! I've never fucked anybody let alone Monte," I blurted out like it was an absurd thought when I had tried to be a ready and willing participant not that long ago.

"Hol' up. You a virgin?" he asked after shuffling up from his wall leaning position in order to give me his full attention.

"Please focus. Who told you I was with Monte like that?"

He hesitated then spoke vaguely until I pretended like I would actually let him take me out if he told me the truth. *Bros over hoes* was suddenly nowhere to be found then.

"A'ight you ain't hear this from me, but it came straight from P."

His words might as well had

been a trigger because they instantly shot me like a bullet across the room over to the exit. Biggs followed closely behind me trying to elaborate, but I only wanted to hear from one person now.

"Hol' up. Wait. Technically he didn't say y'all were getting it in or nothing. He just let niggas know to look but don't touch and we all know what that means. That ain't your girl but that's still *your* girl, know what I mean?"

"Yeah I definitely know what you mean," I told him matter-of-factly before declining to give him my number.

Moe and Jay caught me on

the way out, but I explained that I just needed some fresh air and that I'd be right back. She offered to come with me, but I told her to stay and keep cupcaking with her man since she hardly got to see him as he went to a different school.

I'd never been an expert on walking in heels, but they might as well had been some dunks the way I cleared a path across campus in them. Because mad as hell didn't even begin to explain how I felt. The chill in the air didn't even faze me how it just had on the way in because I was on a mission.

Like the nerve of this nigga

to not only be out here withholding his from me but also blocking me from getting all the other cocks too. He was not playing fair at all and if anything now he actually owed me some type of reparations or back pay dick.

Before approaching their apartment building, I took a deep breath and swore that I wouldn't be too aggressive when I confronted Monte since it had backfired last time. I decided to try a different approach because I knew if I could pull off not blowing up at him then I might just finally get to blow him after all.

It was easier said than done though since I knew I wouldn't be able to stop myself from going for his jugular the second I heard his voice.

"Ay y'all back already?" he yelled out when the front door closed behind me. "Moe?" he called when he got no response but had probably heard me tossing her keys down.

The door to his room had already been wide open so I inconspicuously stood under the arch and watched him hit the punching bag that stood in the corner furthest from the door. Finally he turned and was almost startled when he saw me standing there instead of Moe.

"Ay don't be sneaking up on me like that. Lil' Lee almost got hands put on her," he joked, but I could tell a big part of the surprise was due to how good I looked.

"Well the night is young so you still could if you wanted to. Where would you prefer?" I asked sarcastically as I did a little spin so he could see me from every angle. He responded by rolling his eyes like I was annoying him.

"C'mon Lee, I know you're not still trying to get some dick up off me?" he asked clearly amused with himself and I had to admit that it felt good to see he wasn't sulking even if it was just temporary and at my expense.

"And what if I am?"

"Look I told you to gone somewhere with that shit. Yo lil' fast ass just got off the porch and already don't know how to act." And with that he went back to punching the bag like I wasn't there even as I pulled up a chair to sit in his line of vision.

"Hm. Well I guess I figured it wouldn't hurt to try again since you've been going around telling everybody I've already had it."

My words caused his fist to completely miss the bag as he looked over directly into my eyes. With a smug smile that I'd borrowed from him, I dared him to deny it. "You know I never took you for the type to lie on your dick, but you are just full of surprises these days, *Python*."

"I never said we had sex," he weakly retorted after a few long seconds of silence before shrugging then going back to punching the bag. He was obviously lying like a rug and using semantics to get out of jail free.

"Maybe not directly, but it was still implied."

"Just to protect you."

"Protect me from what, Monte? An orgasm?!" I exclaimed because he sounded ridiculous and I was not in the mood for his games when my reputation was on the line for something that I'd actually wanted to do.

"Lee, you're too green to be with these dirty niggas. I'm doing you a favor so just leave it at that."

"No we won't leave it at that because you're actually doing the opposite of doing me a favor. The only favor I want from you is dick."

The second the words left my lips I was both surprised and a little proud because I had never spoken like that before. Sure I had thought it, but actually standing there and saying exactly what I wanted made me feel powerful as fuck so I continued.

"You don't want me? Cool beans. But we're about to set shit straight around here because I'm grown and I can talk to whoever I want to," I scolded, but I wasn't even sure if he was listening since he couldn't even stop himself from letting his eyes drift down to my angry, heaving chest.

"See that's what I'm talking about! You clearly want to so why can't we just fuck once and get it over with? And do not bring up Moe because you know I wouldn't say shit."

Trying not to run him off again, I slowly stood then approached him again.

Surprisingly he let me get his back up against the wall so I pushed my luck by grabbing hold of his hands and wrapping them around my waist. His breathing had already been a little labored, but he sucked in a big breath of air before slowly letting it out and getting acquainted with the feel of my behind.

For the first time we were both locked in and his lips were finally close enough for me to lick. Feeling victorious but celebrating too soon again, I reached down to feel the only thing that I'd ever wanted to come between us, but he backed up before I could causing me to sigh hard.

"Okay what the fuck is it because now I'm starting to wonder if we're playing for the same team?!" I whined and he just smiled at my frustration which pissed me off because it made him look even cuter.

"Damn, so you think I be out here voguing in my spare time now?" he joked before snapping his fingers in a sassy way.

"No. The way you look at me has always told on you."

"And how do I look at you?" he asked like he didn't already know.

"Like a starving man looks at food," I said to jolt his memory of

Maslow's hierarchy. He knew he couldn't deny it either so he didn't even try to, but he did preemptively back away when I attempted to reel him back in again.

"You know what? Fuck it. I don't even care. I'm probably right and it did finally stop working, huh? That's why you're really being so stingy with it, right?" I teased, trying to use reverse psychology since he had obviously been struggling with the basics.

He had a better understanding than I'd given him credit for though because after stepping back into my personal space and yanking my hand down to let me get a nice grip of his warm stiffness, he said some of the cruelest words my ears had ever heard.

"Trust me, little girl. Not only does it still work, but I promise you it's the best dick you'll **never** have."

THE ENTRÉE

I knew Monte's downward spiral into depression was officially completed when his wardrobe finally went from preppy cardigans and sweater vests to sweatpants and pajamas around the clock. He usually spent a lot of time on his appearance and took pride in being stylish and well groomed, but lately it'd all become more than just an afterthought. It wasn't on the agenda at all.

Even though I had definitely been able to relate to feeling down in the same way before, I would've honestly preferred streaking before showing up in public looking any less than presentable. But that probably had more to do with the spotless but unstable household that I'd been brought up in.

My biological mother had made zero qualms about literally and figuratively beating *cleanliness is next to godliness* into both me and my older sister Lou's heads to the point that losing her actually wasn't too much of a loss; it was more of a relief. In fact I remembered being happy at first because her sudden passing allowed me to finally reunite with Lou since she'd left home years before and never once looked back.

For a while she seemed happy to have me with her too. My niece was still just a toddler then so obviously she didn't have very many rules for her, but I could already see that she would be a different type of parent and guardian to us both. Definitely no beatings and all I had to do to keep her happy was babysit a few hours after school which got annoying sometimes, but overall it had still been the only breathable environment I'd ever lived in.

Every now and then I thought back on those days and wished that even if things couldn't have stayed the same that the good times would've at least lasted a little longer. Because the years in foster care after that may have went by quickly, but the individual days and nights held so much uncertainty that they felt never-ending.

And ever since Homecoming weekend the long nights had seemingly crept back up on me again. I tossed and turned so much that my roommate even showed concern and asked if I was okay. That had been monumental because we'd had a contentious relationship ever since I'd woken up to her getting her spine realigned just a few feet away from me.

Looking back now though I realized that a small part of me may have just been a little envious because it'd sounded like she was having the time of her life underneath those sheets, something I still stupidly longed to experience with Monte. A sane person would've been turned all the way off after getting dissed and dismissed for a second time, but I must've been a masochist because it just seemed to make me crave him even more.

FEAST

It was like my body knew the real thing was finally within reach because even masturbating just hadn't been getting the job done anymore. By the time Thanksgiving break rolled around I was exhausted from sleepless and sexless nights so when Moe told me what time we were supposed to be leaving for her parents' house the following day, I let her know that I'd actually been thinking about sticking around campus for the week.

In my frustrated state, the last thing I'd wanted to do was be forced to spend my break in the same house as Monte pretending that I didn't want him. Since the last mishap we'd kept our distance and really only saw each other in passing, our longest conversations now being *hi* and *bye*, but evidently that was the way it had to be now.

Plus logically it made sense to go ahead and get a jump start to staying on campus for breaks with the international students anyway since I didn't exactly have a family or a home to get back to. Moe didn't want to hear any of that though and immediately accused me of wanting to stay behind because apparently Monte had planned to do the same.

She finally let me know that

she'd been hearing things about us all semester long, but it'd taken her all that time to gather the evidence she needed to actually listen to them.

"You're joking, right? What am I, thirteen again?" I asked trying my best to throw her off my trail. "Ain't nobody thinking about Monte. I just know I can't hang onto your family forever."

"Why not?" she asked like it was an absurd thought.

"Because y'all are already going through a lot right now. And because where am I gonna go when you want to do holidays with Jay's family? Or maybe you won't even want to come home sometimes when you get to D.C. or--"

"Girl if you don't shut yo' ass up!" she interrupted before bursting into laughter, but I couldn't understand why she was being so dismissive until she elaborated. "I was waiting to tell everybody over dinner on Thursday, but since you're moping I guess I can tell you now. I got my acceptance letter for DU Law and I'm thinking maybe I'll stay here and be a Double Demon."

"But what about Howard?" I asked about her dream school since she'd been complaining about the lack of melanin on campus since her freshman year.

"What about it? With everything that's been going on I realized that my mama needs me close and Jay will still be here too," she said about her long-term boyfriend who was only a junior. "But most importantly I don't want to be away from my Little LeeLee anymore. I was even thinking of guilting my daddy into getting us one of the apartments with the jacuzzi tubs next year while he's still in trouble."

Her words left me speechless. It was the best news I'd heard in a while, but I could barely express my excitement because I instantly felt like a bad friend. For months I'd been plotting behind her back to do something I knew she would disapprove of meanwhile she had been making life changing plans with me in mind.

I'd heard that the only thing worse than a strong enemy was a weak friend and my flesh was so weak for Monte that it needed Muscle Milk. That was why as good as the whole thing sounded I let her know that I would be sticking with the dorms next year. I continued lying and said it was because I thought we might clash living together, but she dismissed it and clocked the real reason.

"Monte and his hoes ain't invited. It'll just be me and you," she said before letting it slip that even though he'd gotten into his DU grad program too, he was now thinking of going somewhere else because of the situation with their dad.

Still playing it off, I told her I would still have to put some thought into it before she tried one more time to get me to come home with her.

I didn't regret turning her down until it seemed like all at once that every soul had left campus for the holiday. By Wednesday night it looked like a ghost town and I had foolishly forgotten to get a ride to the store by one of the last shuttles so I could at least attempt to cook something festive. Sure I wouldn't starve because I had enough ramen and pizza rolls to last a lifetime, but that stuff was reserved for late nights after the dining halls were closed, not Thanksgiving.

The snow had been coming down off and on for days too so I didn't even think about chancing getting a cab or food delivery with how bad it looked out my window. But just when I'd admitted defeat and grabbed one of the familiar orange packs from underneath my mid-lofted bed, my Soulja Boy "Kiss Me Through The Phone" ringtone blasted throughout the quiet room.

I had never been so happy to hear from Moe because she hadn't just been calling to check in but to also tell me that her dad was just arriving to campus with dinner for us sent by her mama. Apparently Monte not coming home had left him no choice but to pull up so now everybody was on pins and needles waiting to see how his presence would be received.

Unsurprisingly he stopped by my dorm first and saved his not so mini me across campus for last. Even through the heavy snow flurries and the polite smile on the handsome older man's face, I saw how stressed he looked and wished him good luck after thanking him for dropping off my meal.

Yeah what he'd done could be considered unforgivable, but instead of being home for the holiday he was out in a brewing blizzard trying to make things right with his son. Somehow Monte had become the key to keeping everything together and he seemed to be heading in the right direction by my book.

I still had the chills from the cold air outside as I unpacked my bag of goodies and I didn't know why I'd been expecting Styrofoam plates and aluminum foil like a normal person. Because of course Mrs. McGhee had packed everything up in fancy glass containers meant for reheating in the oven.

Instead of a big, dry, boring bird, she'd gone a little nontraditional with smothered turkey wings, mashed potatoes and gravy, green beans, rolls and half of a pecan pie. It was definitely enough for two portions, but since I would be running through it all at once I decided to shower then jump into my jammies first. A meal like that was capable of tucking me in and with the restless nights I'd been having lately, I welcomed the imminent food coma.

I had barely towel dried my damp body when Soulja Boy started playing again. I figured it was just Moe's mama wanting to know if I enjoyed the food so I thought about calling back after I'd eaten, but by the fourth ring something told me to pick up and it was a good thing I'd listened.

According to Moe the last minute reunion between the McGhee men hadn't gone over well and had actually ended in a huge argument with their dad telling Monte that he wasn't going to be living in an apartment that he paid for while disrespecting him. Monte had surprisingly agreed with the sentiment before storming out and leaving him dumbfounded.

Everybody had been calling Monte nonstop for the last half hour, but he wasn't answering their calls so she wanted to know if I'd heard anything from him. Only the second I opened my mouth to tell her that he hadn't contacted me either, I had a new call coming in.

"Come open the door," his gruff voice shot into the phone without volunteering any other info.

"Why, you finally coming to pay what you owe?" I joked to lighten the air as I went to look out the window for him. Sure enough he was standing in front of Granville Hall wearing the same frown that I'd just heard on the line.

"Ay is your ass in heat or something?" he barked angrily. "Just come open the fucking door!"

"When I fucking feel like it!" I countered, giving him the same attitude before switching back over to Moe.

I could tell that she'd wanted to stay on the line longer to speak to him, but I had never been the best multitasker so I ended the call then purposely took my time putting on my clothes. The loud repetition of knocks that hit my door a few minutes later did nothing to put any pep in my step so when I finally opened the door for a shivering Monte, he didn't look too amused.

Not waiting for an invitation, he rudely pushed past me while letting himself inside.

"Excuse you."

"You're excused," he retorted as he came out of his coat then draped it over the chair to my desk.

"Um you can take that stank attitude back to the same place

you got it from," I informed him as he looked up from taking his shoes off. Chile if looks could kill…

"Lee, I'm really not in the mood for this shit right now."

"Okay and neither am I."

I crossed my arms defensively letting him know that he would decide whether things went smoothly or not because I could go either way with how tense I'd been lately. Knowing that he had nowhere else to go tonight, he sighed then tried to fix his face.

"My dad will be gone in the morning when the roads are clear. I just need somewhere to crash for tonight, alright?"

I almost smiled thinking about our chapter on Maslow and wondered if he would actually be willing to barter a crumb of dick now that he'd suddenly found himself in a situation where he needed shelter. He wore the same stressed expression as his dad though so I decided not to even bother playing with him any further.

I just gave him a pillow and a blanket for the futon since my roommate would have killed me if I let somebody use her bed even though it seemed like half the student body had been in there already.

"So what happened?" I asked him after plopping down on my bed and waiting for the juicy details. I relished in finally being able to get them firsthand instead of watered down and filtered through Moe.

"You know what happened. He fucked around with a bitch that's cool with adultery but draws the line at abortions and my mama's stupid ass is just taking it."

I gave his recap time to breathe because I wasn't used to hearing him talk like that and I needed to find a gentle way to tell him to man the fuck up already.

"Okay don't think I'm

excusing what he did, because I'm not. But I'm just kinda surprised you of all people are giving him a hard time about this because the last time you committed to somebody was…never. I mean how do you think niggas like him *become* niggas like him? They start off as niggas like you, Monte."

"And that's the part everybody's missing. I'm not committed so I can be whatever type of nigga I want to be. He's got a wife who depends on him so he can't. It's that simple."

"Well apparently she's not going anywhere so why are you so upset about it? I mean damn let your mama be dumb in peace," I reasoned because it seemed like it was out of his control regardless, but he still insisted on acting like an emo teenager.

Attempting to reset the conversation before I went to reheat my food in the kitchen, I asked if he had at least enjoyed his meal before they'd started arguing. It ended up being the wrong type of reset though because the instant he told me that he'd thrown it at his father's feet before leaving, I lost the last few marbles I'd been able to hold on to all this time.

"Oh my God. You are so fucking spoiled!" I screamed as I

neared his confused face. "I wouldn't have brought your ungrateful ass shit. You don't show up. You don't eat! You got a chip on your shoulder because your family's not perfect. Well guess what? At least you have a family to even disappoint you. I don't even have that! Look where the fuck I am, Monte. Alone and in a dorm on Thanksgiving with a pack of noodles and not by fucking choice like your dumb ass! Because where else am I gonna fucking go when I'm not pretending to be a McGhee, huh?"

I punctuated my rant by slamming the tops back on the food containers because just that quickly he had made me lose my fucking appetite. I was so angry I could cry and I couldn't stop myself from hurling more insults his way as I put everything away in the mini fridge. Despite this he still came over and tried to console me only I shrugged him off.

"Don't fucking touch me!" I snatched away as he tried to pull me into one of the hugs I'd foolishly let him know I enjoyed so much.

"Okay, but what if I said that I was ready to fuck now? Could I touch you then?" he asked casually like he wasn't suddenly saying exactly what I'd been begging him to say for weeks.

My lips were pursed together so they definitely didn't ask him anything, but he seemed to be answering the question asked by my bewildered eyes.

"Are they still teaching y'all HALT for freshman orientation?" he asked coming out of left field. I nodded thinking back to the stressor acronym which stood for *Hungry Angry Lonely Tired*.

"Yeah well I'm all four right now and I could really go for some sweet pussy in my mouth and on my dick to make me forget about this shit for a minute. Are you down?"

The heat had been on full

blast like it always was in the building, but I swore I felt frozen where I stood. We held eye contact the whole time I thawed though so I saw him smirk when he thought he had me, but I'd finally located just enough dignity to turn him down. He didn't agree to give me the no strings attached dick that I'd wanted before so now I wouldn't let him turn me into stress relief pussy on a whim.

"No. Don't nobody want you or your ashy dick anymore. I'm going to bed." I attempted to go lie down, but he put an arm out to make sure I was certain.

"Going once, going twice," he

teased causing me to crack a smile against my will.

"Going to bed," I repeated as I pushed past his arm then proceeded to lay my head down on my pillows.

He seemed to accept my decision and was taking it in stride, but ten minutes into turning out the lights then five more into an episode of *The Nanny* on Nick At Nite and I heard him almost moaning my name from the futon.

"Lee, c'mon. You know I didn't come all this way just to get away from my dad, right?"

It had been too soon to pretend like I'd fallen asleep so I

didn't even try. I just flat out ignored him the same way he'd done me because I wanted him to feel exactly like I had when he'd denied me before.

"Okay how about this then? You don't have to let me touch you. Just let me see you touch yourself for a little while," he offered as an alternative. "They say if you want something done right, you gotta do it yourself anyway, right? Well I know nobody knows that little pussy like you do so show me what you can do with it real quick."

I planned to keep on ignoring him. I really did. But one glance in his direction nearly took my breath away. Aside from the obvious comedy troupe reference, the fistful of impressive veiny dick made me see why they called him Python. And watching him shine it up with his own spit had me finally ready to get on the naughty list this year.

In one swift motion I lifted my butt to completely rid me of my pajama bottoms. I was still too shy to take off my panties, but he didn't seem to mind as I was still spread eagled in seconds and circling my clit while staring into his soul.

I saw his breath get caught in his throat and smiled when it made his Adam's apple and his dick bob up and down.

"Tell me you still want me to fuck you," he groaned out as he suddenly began pumping faster at the sight of me in front of him.

That made me push my fingers deeper than I'd ever pushed them, attempting to reach where we both wanted him to plant himself. I knew if I repeated after him though that I would lose what little power I still had left, but I didn't care anymore. I did want him to fuck me so I told him so.

"I still want you to fuck me so bad, Monte," I moaned out and realized that simply having him there with me made everything feel really good again.

"I know you do. But I ain't with that soft shit, Lee. If I come over there, no mercy for the inexperienced, a'ight? I fuck you, you better fuck me back. You hear me?"

"I promise! Monte please! I promise I'll fuck you back!" I exclaimed as my body began to spasm uncontrollably.

It was the fastest I'd ever brought myself to my peak and not long after he released, shooting several big spurts at least three feet above him before they splash landed on his stomach. I had never seen anything like that before and if his dad was anything like him then I could see how he was still out here knocking women up at his age because geesh.

As I laid back trying to suck in small puffs of air, I realized how embarrassed I was at where my hand still was and how wet it'd gotten so fast, but I still couldn't break eye contact with him.

Obviously we'd both taken good care of ourselves already so I wondered if that would just be the end of it. I got my answer when he took off his wifebeater and used it to clean himself up then walked over to me. Yeah it definitely wasn't the end, I noted as he fully stepped out of his sweatpants then presented himself to me as naked as the day he was born.

"Is your mouth a virgin too?" he asked curiously as he pulled on his semi hard length in my face and I nodded. "Good. Get on your knees."

He'd barely finished the command and I was already on all fours, all too eager to do exactly what he wanted me to do. My mouth had been watering just thinking about feeling him slide back and forth between every opening my body would allow.

"That's a good girl. You real thankful for this dick, ain't you?" he asked in a teasing tone causing even more of the moisture inside of me to become displaced.

He then waited until my tongue made deliberate and extended contact with the underside to admonish me.

"Rookie mistake. Always make a nigga taste you first. That way you can see if it's even worth returning the favor."

"I knew that," I said defiantly as he pressed his warm, spongey flesh into my lips.

"Sure you did. And watch your teeth. Don't scrape my shit."

"Don't try to gag me and I

won't," I warned before softly slurping on the tip. It still wasn't all the way hard again, but it felt good in my mouth so I savored it.

"Nah I'mma have to be gentle with that pussy at first, but your mouth is fair game. Open that shit up. And keep playing with your pussy while you're at it," he instructed as he put my hand back on my clit.

"I want it dripping so get it wet for me." I did exactly what he told me to and before long he was coming back to life between my lips.

"Fuck. This dick ain't so ashy now, is it? My shit moisturized as fuck now, ain't it?" he asked rhetorically since it was obvious that I loved having my mouth too full to answer.

I'd never been into video games too much, but I treated him like a joystick and toyed around until I found the right combo for a knockout. And by no means was I an expert already, but just keeping a steady rhythm while staring up into his eyes seemed to be enough to get the job done.

After a little while of that though I got bored and decided to experiment and switch things up, causing him to look down at me with a peculiar expression.

"Are you trying to spell your

name on my dick?" he asked easily deciphering the Da Vinci code I'd thought I was laying out. I had no choice but to finally use my hands as I laughed and confirmed his suspicions.

"Yeah but I'm fancy so it's in cursive," I joked before he quickly reinserted himself with a groan.

"Lee's too short. Use your middle and last name too and don't forget to dot your I's," he instructed before I just skipped to swirling my tongue around in his slit.

That immediately made him hiss and stumble backwards until he popped clean out of my mouth. I went to recapture him with my lips, but I was too late and he'd already turned his attention to what I had going on below the waist.

"Wait why are you still wearing these? Get up and let me see what you got for me," he requested with a distinctly ravenous lick of his lips. Feeling shy again, I slowly stood then shimmied out of my panties.

"Hurry up!" he growled impatiently then followed it up with a stinging slap on my bare butt.

"I am! Wait a second."

"What, you got a little forest down there or something? The carpet matches the drapes?" he cracked about the bushy hair on top of my head.

"No! I just shaved the other day." I'd went to finally get waxed with Moe but chickened out at the last minute like always and instead trimmed it down into a cute little triangle.

"I mean it's cool if you do. You can let your soul glow with me."

"Monte, shut up!"

"I will when you move your hand. Let me see."

After taking a deep breath, I laid back down across the middle of my bed then bared the most private part of me. His eyes widened then narrowed as he looked back and forth from me to my puffy wet folds a couple times.

"Okay Lee! Look at you," he said sounding impressed as he dropped down to his knees. I almost blushed but full on laughed at what he said next. "I'm 'bout to spit some Twista lyrics in this pretty motherfucker."

It was amazing how literally putting some pussy in his face already had him acting like his normal, goofy self again. To think if he would've just given in weeks ago I could've been pulled him out of his funk.

He left me no time to ponder the *what ifs* though because he dove right in, teasing my clit with the tip of his tongue. I was impatient and wanted him to suck on it right away, but he seemed to like playing around with his food for a while first.

"Damn I thought you might need a spit start but you're already wet as fuck just from sucking on me. I knew you were a nasty little bitch," he complimented in a strange degrading way, but the way my body responded to his words told him how much I liked it.

I was so turned on that I started pinching my own nipples through my shirt until he saw what I was doing and got distracted. It was like a lightbulb went off and he realized that he'd been so concerned with my pussy that he had forgotten all about the set of twins on my chest.

He couldn't have gotten my shirt off any quicker if he'd tried. Still he attempted to be conservative at first, toying with the tip of my nipples only, but by the time he accepted his fate he gave in to his wants and inhaled as much as he could get in his mouth. He got comfortable and rested his weight on me then sloppily sucked me for all I was worth.

I instinctively supported his head as he went back and forth because I'd had no idea that just getting my nipples sucked could feel so damn good.

"Damn you always did have some big, juicy ass titties," he said stopping to admire them as he came up for air, but he was in such a trance that he started talking to himself. "Shoulda been did this shit. What the fuck was I thinking?"

I could tell that it would be a little while longer before I would be able to pry him off my chest, but at that point my body was so hot that it was yearning to finally feel any part of him inside of me. I took one of his hands and told him I was holding it hostage between my legs until he got me off again. He just lazily grinned before tracing my slick lips with two larger than expected fingers.

"You think you might bleed?"

"No, I do it all the time." He smirked at my honesty.

"Thinking about me, huh?"

A quick nod was all I could get out because that was when he decided to stimulate me with his mouth while also stroking my core with precision. And like I'd mentioned my fingers were no stranger to the area, but his felt like somebody's who were almost masters of the lost art. He was clearly just touching my body, but a different type of storm than the one outside was building inside of me.

I turned to the side, searching for an escape to get away from how good it all felt. My eyes were already in the back of my head, but he used his strength to hold my body in place.

"Nah where you going? We're just getting warmed up. You can't tap out yet. This what you wanted, right?" he asked as he reacquainted his mouth with my clit then lapped up every drop that trickled down because of him.

"Wait stop. Stop! It feels too good!" I yelled out when I finally found my voice again, but he just chuckled at my dramatics.

"It's supposed to."

"Monte stop. Please. I gotta peeee!" I warned him repeatedly but him knowing better than me kept sucking and stroking until my hips wildly bucked every which way.

I'd skillfully made myself climax for years now, but in the history of all my busted nuts I had never went SPLAT like the damn Nickelodeon logo. I gushed so much that he was left drenched and dripping, but even that couldn't stop him from eating so long that the concept of leftovers sounded like a made up myth from some far away land.

FEAST

It was a happy meal if I'd ever seen one and now I too was having the time of my life and I owed it all to him.

I laid there for a while, spent but still spread as wide as all outside and not fully believing that it was Monte McGhee's mouth on my body with a tongue that was just as skilled and diligent as his fingers. I couldn't fathom his dick game being whack, but even if it turned out to be he had already done enough to pass with flying colors.

I quickly raised my head from its flat position when I felt him climbing into bed with me. Because I was out of it, but not that out of it to realize that he wasn't wearing any protection and I wasn't taking any chances since the McGhee men obviously weren't shooting blanks these days.

In all the scenarios I'd imagined over the last few weeks I didn't have to worry about supplying a condom since we were doing things in his apartment where I had seen his stash in the bathroom he shared with Moe. And the only ones that I'd ever had access to were the freebies in the communal bathrooms, but I was sure that they had all been cleaned and cleared for the break.

Without skipping a beat and proving that he really was his daddy's son, he assured me that it was fine to go without one because...

"I always strap up."

"Let's keep it that way then," I said putting on my no nonsense voice before we engaged in a stare off.

I knew the idea of trekking back out in the snow to get one was not appealing, but it was his only option unless he wanted to use his hand again. He kissed his teeth when he saw that as much as I wanted it, this was something that I wouldn't be budging on. He stood from the bed then suddenly started rummaging through the things on top of my roommate's desk.

"What are you doing?"

"This is where she keeps them," he said casually then celebrated as he found a three pack with two still inside.

"And how do you know that?" I stupidly asked when the answer was literally swinging right in front of me as he opened the packaging with his teeth then expertly slid it on.

"Don't ask. Don't tell."

"But I thought you didn't fuck with 'little girls' like me. She's two months younger than me," I retorted, sounding more childish and jealous than I'd wanted to appear while moving back into a vertical position on the bed.

"You're a little girl who's a virgin and you're Moe's people. That's three strikes. She only had one. Now close your mouth and open your legs," he rudely instructed while lining himself up with my body.

For a minute I stopped to imagine how thirteen year old Lee would feel about this exact situation going so completely different than how she'd hyped it up in her mind back then. Because she'd had sexy music playing, rose petals scattered about and candles lighting up the room.

All we had was the glare from my small TV and the sounds of Jodeci were replaced with Fran Drescher's nasally laughter in the background. It had oddly put me at ease though and took away a lot of the pressure I'd felt about sex so I wouldn't have changed a thing.

One determined push and he was in. I was still gushy wet so without the resistance that dryness could cause he forged on until he couldn't anymore. That was when I had to ease back for my own comfort.

"Wait. Just. Shit!" I complained because it seemed

like he had gotten even bigger than my mouth remembered.

"Aht aht. This what you wanted, big girl. Keep it right there," he urged but did the right thing and withdrew some. "You're lucky I got manners. I ain't gon start off beating your shit up, but I do want to bury it so keep up."

He'd talked a good game all night, but the short, slow strokes he followed up with seemed like he was moreso trying to concentrate on not coming too fast.

"How does it feel?" I asked since he was moving so timidly that I couldn't really tell if I liked it or not.

"Good," he said simply.

"Just good? Not the best you ever had?" He suddenly pulled his face from my neck then smiled down at me.

"You feel real good, Lee," he complimented, "Even with this fucking raincoat on," he complained as he finally pushed in further, causing me to wince again as my body tried to accommodate him. "It hurts?" he asked as he came to a complete stop, but I shook my head no and urged him to keep going.

"Not really. I guess I just feel real full when you do that."

"Just full? Not stuffed and stretched?" he asked mocking me.

"Definitely not stuffed and stretched," I cracked.

"What about now?" he asked before letting himself sink in some more, but I couldn't have responded if I wanted to. Like a power button, he'd touched something that made my left leg violently shake with a strong tremor.

We locked eyes as he moved to hit it again. My body had the same reaction. That was all it took for him to really put his back into the next few strokes and my lower half, now with a mind of its own almost lifted his off the bed reaching up to meet him halfway in an erotic push and pull motion.

"There we go. You like that shit, don't you?" he asked as we began to develop a steady rhythm. "Lil' Lee is all grown up now and out here taking dick like a boss."

Yeah so it was a wrap after that. I followed his lead and talked back even though I didn't know where the nasty ass words were coming from. Because certainly not from my innocent brain. And despite knowing that we had a barrier of protection between us, I begged this man to somehow finish inside of me.

His body instantly tightened at the words so I wrapped him in my legs and held on for dear life as he began plunging hard dick into my center and soul with the vigor of a beast.

Blow by blow, it got so good that he became incoherent so his moans and well-saturated strokes had to do the talking for him. But as for me, I couldn't do anything but lay there and take the grown man dick that he'd so thoughtfully warned me about before.

And as my body started to frantically clench again, my mind began its official descent into madness. Being stretched and stuffed to the hilt by a Sigma man had even managed to bring out my own sudden appreciation for

Lil' Wayne because as Monte hit the kill switch, I could now confirm that **that** really was how you let the beat build, bitch.

THE DESSERT

Staring up at the popcorn ceiling in my room was something I usually only did when I either couldn't fall asleep fast enough or if I had woken up early before my alarm could go off. It was almost identical to the bedroom I had growing up, but the green glow in the dark stars that were stuck on that ceiling were why my eyes were always fixed upwards then.

It had seemed like just

yesteryear that I'd spent Thanksgivings cutting out then coloring hand-traced turkeys to now spending the holiday finding out what it was like to get stuffed like a real one. The latter was definitely a tradition that I could get used to though.

It took a while to accept that I hadn't just been vividly dreaming about my first sexual encounter with Monte, but his very real and heavy body still resting between my thighs was more proof than a simple pinch could ever produce.

"Are you ever gonna get off me?" I whined as I wiggled underneath him.

"No. I'm getting you a cap and gown too because they're gonna have to tear me off you to walk across the stage," he said sounding half-serious through a groan before our bodies shook from my laughter.

Finally he did a long and dramatic stretch before rolling over on his side. The twin sized bed hadn't seemed all that small a second ago when we were stacked up together like Legos, but now that we were side by side its limited spatial density became more apparent.

One of us would have to go soon and it certainly wasn't going to be me, but his stellar performance had bought him a few more minutes of rest and recovery time.

I had only closed my eyes for a second when I felt a finger playfully tapping my nose.

"Go pee before you fall asleep. That's important."

"I knew that too," I yawned out. "I was going."

My Bambi walk over to the bathroom should have come as no surprise since he'd just cracked my legs open like I was a snow crab, but the mild ache and tenderness I felt when I sat down to pee really made me think about what I'd just done.

Aside from looking tired and

my hair being messier than it'd been earlier, my reflection in the mirror didn't appear much different. But then again I had looked like a woman for longer than even I could process. Mentally though, I'd accepted that I still resided in that weird in between space that Britney Spears had sang about years ago.

Halfway through an intentionally ironic hummed rendition of "I'm Not a Girl, Not Yet a Woman", my bathroom solitude was interrupted by a boxer clad Monte coming to discard the condom in the trash.

"Are you lost? The men's room is on the floor below," I said sarcastically because it wasn't like there were any RAs or even students on my floor left behind to catch him.

"I thought about going down there, but then I heard you in here singing. I don't think I've ever made anybody do that before so I had to come see it for myself."

I was too tired to even think of a comeback so I just let him gloat in peace before taking one of the small towels that he'd helped himself to from my room. Too exhausted to shower, I did a quick but thorough hoe bath so I could hurry and get back into bed.

"So how many times have you lied about being a virgin?"

The question itself hadn't caught me off guard, but combined with the casual way he'd made the accusation I took a second to think about my answer.

"Wow. You've been around the block so many times that you can actually tell. I'm impressed."

"Nah it wasn't anything physical. You were tighter than OJ's glove," he said mannishly with a quick lick of his lips. "You just didn't really act like a virgin."

"Well what does a virgin act like?" I asked curiously since I hadn't actually been one in a while, but he couldn't pinpoint anything specific to give a real answer. "Right. For all intents and purposes let's just say I was born again and restored with a virgin heart. Problem solved."

His eyebrow rose, but before he could poke any holes in the statement I left the bathroom and hoped that it would be the end of it. I grabbed an oversized t-shirt from my drawer to throw on then internally debated if going commando would be best after all the friction I'd just experienced.

"Ay Lee, that's bullshit and you know it," he said as soon as he stepped back into the room. There was no clear motive though because it didn't sound like he was disappointed that he wasn't actually my first. He just seemed to want clarity.

"I've known you for how long now and I ain't never known you to go to church."

"Yeah I don't anymore, but I practically lived there as a kid so like every other part-time believer I lean into my faith whenever shit gets real," I said honestly before letting my eyes fall from his, but before they reached my hands I saw him finally nod, fully grasping the meaning behind my words.

"So it was the first time you got to choose then?" he asked directly and I slowly nodded as I finally turned off the TV but then replaced the light with the dim lamp next to my bed.

I was relieved that he wasn't as dumb as he acted sometimes and had put two and two together on his own because I really didn't want to get into all the details of how I had ended up in foster care for a little while after my mama had died.

And I would have rather twisted myself into a pretzel than to have to explain how my sister Lou, my rescuer, had essentially put me back into the system when my presence in her home became an inconvenience. It'd taken years, but I'd finally found a polite and concise way to say that she had fought me like I was a stranger in the street after finding the evidence of what my niece's dad, her boyfriend, had been doing to me.

Ever since I could remember my vocabulary had been described as vast by those around me, but back then I didn't have the words to say that I was uncomfortable with the weird jokes he started telling when my sister wasn't around. Or how icky I felt when he would point out the differences between our body shapes. Or how my skin crawled whenever he found an excuse to touch me.

Neither Lou nor myself had

any idea what grooming was then, but yeah he had groomed me. And he'd done such a good job at it that for years I internalized it and blamed myself. For a while I couldn't even get mad at Lou because from her point of view she had left home early to escape our mother's abuse and then I came along and ruined the happy little family she had tried to build by enticing her man with the well-developed body parts that she herself hadn't inherited.

Aside from the therapist I'd been mandated to see back in the day, I had never talked to anybody about the things I'd experienced during the time I spent in Lou's care. Moe didn't even know that I had family outside of a deceased mother and I preferred it that way.

Because while my life thus far hadn't been the easiest, I still had a lot to be thankful for and I didn't ever want to be permanently stained with all the fucked up shit that'd happened to me. Sure it was all a part of my story, but I liked to view it like it was the basket of bread placed on the table before the main courses came out.

Of course it was a part of the meal too, but it would never be more memorable or important than what a person chose to put into their body after that.

"So you finally got to choose and you chose me?" Monte asked curiously, nearly startling me because I'd almost forgotten he was there until he'd spoken.

I nodded again causing an errant tear to fall, but I swiped it away before it could have an effect on the conversation.

"You got something else you want to tell me?" he asked straightforwardly, but my cheeks swelling into a genuine smile opened the floodgates to my eyes and the saltwater trickled down my face.

"No. I swear I'm not going soft on you. In fact you were only chosen because everybody knows the fastest way to get rid of you is to give you some coochie," I joked and he cracked a smile. "But at the same time I knew you were somebody that I could trust because you've always looked out for me even when you didn't have to."

"Yeah I'm starting to wonder if maybe that was because I had sensed something from you that had been in me too," he said vaguely before coming to take a seat near me at my desk.

"I was eight," he volunteered with his back to me, responding to the silent question I wouldn't have dared to ask him out loud.

"What about you?"

"Thirteen," I said after a long sigh because until that moment it'd never dawned on me that I never had the privilege of thinking of it as a lucky number.

That was when he turned to look at me over his shoulder, probably thinking that my experiences hadn't taken place too long before he'd met me.

I hadn't been too surprised at his revelation though because I had always been suspicious that he'd gone through some early trauma too and it certainly would've explained how hypersexual he'd been up until recently. We'd just responded to everything differently.

While I had mostly kept myself sequestered from boys until I felt ready, he'd drowned himself in girls to prove that he was a **real man** and incapable of being abused. But of course the mindfuck of it all was that while his genitals had certainly grown to adulthood, his mind and heart still had a lot of catching up to do.

I hadn't been expecting Mr. No Soft Shit to reach back to gently brush aside my still damp from sweat hair or then take it upon himself to handle the few fresh tears that I had yet to wipe. But the most unexpected part was when he turned around in his chair so that he was able to kiss my lips.

It was weird at first because I realized that even with as much as we'd just done with and to each other that we hadn't bothered letting our lips get acquainted in the least bit. He really got into it too and before long he was standing and trying to get me to lay back down.

"No I'm tired," I yawned out, finally breaking contact with his mouth. "I've had enough of you for a lifetime but especially for tonight," I joked because as much as I'd enjoyed myself I couldn't imagine making it through another round.

"But I need you to be born again one more time for me. Your first time shouldn't have been like that either," he reasoned, being sweeter than I'd ever seen from him, but I didn't need or want a pity party. I was fine.

I didn't want things to suddenly get intense so I just reminded him that we'd said it would just be one time only.

"Yeah one time fucking, right? Now I want one time of what it's supposed to be like," he said before walking over to get another condom without me needing to insist again.

That small gesture made me pull my shirt back over my head

before turning off the light and making room for him in bed again. Our noses touched as we laid there innocently kissing for a little while, both pretending that our bodies had never been taken advantage of as we prepared to give each other the first time we deserved.

Everything was going fine, but I heard the tires screech in my head when he told me to get on top. I instantly looked at him like he had grown another head because he knew I was not ready for all that just yet, but even in the dark I could make out that gorgeous, persuasive grin on his face.

"C'mon, I'mma help you. Just get on and grind or bounce, whatever feels better to you."

I liked the sound of that so I decided to give it a try, but looking down at him from the dominant position was something I would have to get used to. It must've been weird for him too because before entering me again he sat up so that we were face to face then kept his promise by putting both hands on my waist to guide me.

"You got it. Mm. Just like that, Lee," he encouraged as I began to do a poor imitation of Shakira and pretended that my hips didn't lie either.

Our lips locked again, but finding their way back together did nothing to stop him from being just as talkative as he'd been all night. Only now the crude language from before had been replaced with him telling me how perfect I was.

Over and over my moans were met with hearing how good I felt and tasted. How thankful he was to be inside of me and how it was the best gift he'd ever gotten. I almost let it overwhelm me before I remembered that this was how first times were supposed to be.

Only I didn't bother wondering if he meant any of it.

Instead I just enjoyed the moment and being with somebody who cared enough to take their time with me.

After a while of the super sweet stuff though I felt myself wanting to get back to basics and leaned forward to create a longer stroke between us. I almost let him slip out before quickly slamming backwards to gobble him up again and again. He clearly liked the training wheels being off just as much as I had so he finally moved his hands to let me go at it alone.

"That's all you now. You're doing it," he said proudly while letting his fingertips find my breasts again. "First time out and you're already riding it like you don't want to share."

"Oh please. Your dick practically has 'Share Size' stamped on it like candy."

He just smirked before telling me not to worry about that anymore because it was all mine now. I couldn't tell if he'd meant *now* as in *here and now*, the actual present moment or going forward altogether, but I did know that hearing him say it made me come so hard that he had to hold onto me to make sure I didn't fall off.

He continued to rock my body from underneath until it brought him to another toe curling finish. He'd buried his head in my neck again, but I was able to make out him saying that I felt so good that it would be worth getting his ass beat if Moe ever found out. I was positive that he'd never been threatened as he'd came before, but as I finished milking him for all he was worth I let him know that he did not ever want to see the side of me that would come out if he ever told a soul about us.

After getting cleaned up for a second time we realized that we had almost completed HALT except for still being hungry and tired. Unlike him though I still had my leftovers in the fridge and he was lucky that not only was there enough but that I actually was in the mood to share. Because letting him starve would have been a well-deserved lesson after how childish he'd been to waste his.

We were too lazy to bring down any plates so after heating everything up in the oven, we carefully sat at the counter and ate directly from the hot glass containers. Our conversation managed to roll bounce all over the place like Sweetness before he asked if I would still be coming home with Moe for Christmas break.

"I don't know. Do you think you can stand being around all of this and not doing anything?" I asked sarcastically though I was interested to see how he acted towards me going forward.

"Now that you mention it I don't know how I feel about bringing you around my dad for too long. He's in enough trouble as it is," he said finally thinking about the situation with some levity.

"Listen I didn't want to say nothing, but I see why he's still in these streets. And he's the one with all the money? I definitely went after the wrong McGhee," I joked before getting poked in the side with his plastic fork.

We continued talking about everything and nothing at all while I mostly picked over what was left on my side. Everything tasted really good, but watching him eat became more interesting when I saw that he'd made the same satisfied faces as he had when I'd just been on his tongue. I just smiled and kept it to myself though.

"Did Moe tell you I got into my grad program here?" he asked out of the blue.

"Yeah I think I did hear something about you trying to be a Double Demon too. But why are you telling *me* this? I know you're not trying to go soft on me?"

"Me? Soft? Nah," he repeated like there was anything but a little truth to the statement. "I'm just letting you know that I'll still be around if you ever need somebody to talk to. Somebody who gets it."

"Thanks, but you need to be using those communication skills to talk to your dad because you will not be staying here the rest of the week," I joked to keep the conversation on a lighter note before realizing that there was one more important thing to address first.

"And then maybe after that we can both go talk to one of the counselors here about all the stuff we've been holding close to our chests."

"I'm good. I don't need it," he protested before I gave him my theory of why the sudden potential decline of his parents' marriage had affected him so much over the course of the semester.

I guessed that it was because he'd buried his trauma to keep not just his own but also his family's image together, but all these years later it seemed to be coming apart anyway.

"Alright. I'll go if you go," he relented after telling me that I really should pursue a psych major since I had come in completely undecided but obviously connected with it so much.

And just like the kids at heart that we both still were, we made a promise to do so with our pinkies, but after taking another long look at each other we had one final sweet kiss on the lips.

When he'd stepped in to help me straighten up my bed, I'd assumed it was just because he had taken part in messing it up, but of course it'd been because he wanted to get back in it too. I was adamantly against it, sure that there was no way we'd both be able to sleep comfortably in such a tiny space. He just shrugged then claimed that we would make it work before draping an arm over then cuddling up behind me.

And it would've been a lie to say that sharing a pillow with and finally being in my old crush's arms didn't feel right for the night, but ultimately I knew it could never happen again and as I drifted off with his warm breath on my face I realized that I really was okay with it.

Of course it also helped that I didn't suddenly feel some deep love awaken inside of me just because we'd spent one cool night together. He was still "ain't shit" ass Monte and part of his allure was even gone after scratching that long-awaited itch I'd had for him. But in its place there was now a new understanding and appreciation of him that I was sure would stick with me for a while.

Only I would do everything in my power to never let it interfere with the sisterhood I'd built with Moe over the years. Because from the first day we'd met, she had been the friend I'd always needed and not even wanting to fuck her brother as bad as I had would've been worth losing her.

Especially when she'd just rightfully wanted something for herself since she always had to share everything she had with him. Birthdays. Friends. Hell their face. But unbeknownst to her in the morning after walking him out, I would revert right back to just being hers.

I was thankful that I'd found a way to have my feast and eat it too and that finally at eighteen I really was becoming mature enough to be able to push the plate back when I'd had just enough.

FEAST

FOLLOW ME

Thanks for reading! If you don't want to miss out on any updates about future works of mine then find me on all social media platforms as TanSaidWhat, sign up for my mailing list and join my reading group Turning The Page With Tanzania Glover.

Visit www.tanzaniaglover.com

And if the cover art took your breath away as much as it did mine, check out the talented

artist Scheba Derogene! Thank
you so much for bringing this
couple to life!

TANZANIA GLOVER